Clifford's™ puppy days

GRADUATION PARTY

by Victoria Kosara

Illustrated by Jim Durk

Based on the Scholastic book series
"Clifford The Big Red Dog"
by Norman Bridwell

ISBN 978-0-545-23400-9

Designed by Michael Massen

12 11 10 9 8 7 6 5 4 3 2 1   10 11 12 13 14 15/0

Printed in the U.S.A.

First printing, May 2010   40

SCHOLASTIC INC.

New York   Toronto   London   Auckland
Sydney   Mexico City   New Delhi   Hong Kong

Clifford loved to play outside in the warm spring weather. The sun was shining. It was almost summer.

Mr. and Mrs. Howard took Clifford for a
walk in the park. They liked spring, too. But
they couldn't stay long.

"Come on, Clifford!" said Mr. and
Mrs. Howard. "Let's get ready for Emily
Elizabeth's graduation."

Clifford was not sure what they meant.
He went to ask some of his friends.

Clifford found Flo and Zo on his way inside. "We took obedience lessons," Flo and Zo told Clifford. "When we graduated, we had a party!"

A party sounded good, but Clifford still was not sure what graduation meant.

Clifford went to the laundry room and
found the Sidarskys. "When people graduate
from school," said Mrs. Sidarsky, "they wear a
special hat."

Hats and parties sounded fun. Clifford
wanted to know what else happened at a
graduation. He couldn't wait to ask Jorgé at
the dog park.

"Hola, Jorgé!" Clifford said. Then Clifford asked Jorgé about graduation.

"All the friends and family of the graduate come to watch her get her diploma. There is a speech, and everyone claps," Jorgé told Clifford.

When Clifford passed through the kitchen,
Mr. and Mrs. Howard were painting a big
sign. It said *Congratulations!*
Clifford went to find Daffodil.

"Daffodil," Clifford asked, "what happens at a graduation? I know there is a party and special hats. What else is there?"

Daffodil thought for a moment.

"You get a diploma when you graduate. It's a rolled-up piece of paper with a pretty bow. The diploma says you did it!" Daffodil said.

Clifford thought about all the things that made up a graduation. "What does a graduation look like?" he asked.

"That's a good question," said Daffodil. "Let's find all the things you heard about so you'll be ready for Emily Elizabeth's graduation tomorrow."

Clifford was excited.

First Clifford asked the Sidarskys to help
him make a graduation hat.
It looked great!

Next Jorgé helped Clifford to roll up a diploma.

"That looks just right!" Daffodil said.

Last, Daffodil helped Clifford add his own
special touch to the banner that Mr. and Mrs.
Howard had made.

Everything looked so exciting.

Clifford couldn't wait to go to

Emily Elizabeth's graduation.

When Emily Elizabeth came home, she saw Clifford with the hat, banner, and diploma that he had made with his friends. She smiled.

"Oh, Clifford!" she said. "Is this for my graduation party? I feel so special!" She bent down and patted Clifford.

At Emily Elizabeth's graduation ceremony, Clifford was happy. It was so nice to celebrate the special people in your life with everyone you love.

When the ceremony was over, everybody went back to the Howards' to party.

"Congratulations, Emily Elizabeth!" everyone shouted.

Everyone smiled. It was a perfect day to celebrate being special.